A Moose in a Maple Tree

THE ALL-CANADIAN 12 DAYS OF CHRISTMAS

Cover Design by Jennifer Harrington

Printed in Canada by Friesens

Library and Archives Canada Cataloguing in Publication

Townsin, Troy, 1975-
        A moose in a maple tree : the all-Canadian 12 days of Christmas / by
Troy Townsin ; illustrated by Jennifer Harrington.

ISBN 978-0-9737748-6-3

1. Twelve days of Christmas (English folk song)--Adaptations.
2. Christmas--Juvenile fiction. 3. Picture books for children.
I. Harrington, Jennifer, 1973- II. Title.

PS8639.O998M65 2008   jC813'.6   C2007-905920-1

A Moose in a Maple Tree

THE ALL-CANADIAN 12 DAYS OF CHRISTMAS

By Troy Townsin

Illustrated by Jennifer Harrington

www.polyglotpublishing.com

On the first day of Christmas,
a Canuck sent to me
a moose in a maple tree.

On the second day of Christmas,
a Canuck sent to me
2 polar bears
and a moose in a maple tree.

On the third day of Christmas,

a Canuck sent to me

3 snowmen

2 polar bears

and a moose in a maple tree.

On the fourth day of Christmas,

a Canuck sent to me

4 totem poles

3 snowmen

2 polar bears

and a moose in a maple tree.

On the fifth day of Christmas,

a Canuck sent to me

5 hockey sticks

4 totem poles

3 snowmen

2 polar bears

and a moose in a maple tree.

On the sixth day of Christmas,

a Canuck sent to me

6 whales breaching

5 hockey sticks

4 totem poles

3 snowmen

2 polar bears

and a moose in a maple tree.

On the seventh day of Christmas,

a Canuck sent to me

7 beavers building

6 whales breaching

5 hockey sticks

4 totem poles

3 snowmen

2 polar bears

and a moose in a maple tree.

On the eighth day of Christmas,

a Canuck sent to me

8 lobsters nipping

7 beavers building

6 whales breaching

5 hockey sticks

4 totem poles

3 snowmen

2 polar bears

and a moose in a maple tree.

On the ninth day of Christmas,

a Canuck sent to me

9 mounties riding

8 lobsters nipping

7 beavers building

6 whales breaching

5 hockey sticks

4 totem poles

3 snowmen

2 polar bears

and a moose in a maple tree.

On the tenth day of Christmas,

a Canuck sent to me

10 salmon leaping

9 mounties riding

8 lobsters nipping

7 beavers building

6 whales breaching

5 hockey sticks

4 totem poles

3 snowmen

2 polar bears

and a moose in a maple tree.

On the eleventh day of Christmas,
a Canuck sent to me
11 sled dogs mushing
10 salmon leaping
9 mounties riding
8 lobsters nipping
7 beavers building
6 whales breaching
5 hockey sticks
4 totem poles
3 snowmen
2 polar bears
and a moose in a maple tree.

On the twelfth day of Christmas,
a Canuck sent to me

12 skiers skiing

11 sled dogs mushing

10 salmon leaping

9 mounties riding

8 lobsters nipping

7 beavers building

6 whales breaching

5 hockey sticks

4 totem poles

3 snowmen

2 polar bears

AND...

a moose in a maple tree!

This book is dedicated to the people of Canada and to all those who visit this wonderful country.

Partial proceeds from the sale of this book have been donated to Make-A-Wish® Canada.

ABOUT THE AUTHOR

Troy Townsin is a proud new Canadian!

Born in Melbourne, Australia he worked as an actor and playwright before embarking on a round-the world backpacking extravaganza taking him to several continents. Troy has had many jobs. He has been a Stage Manager in Australia, a Teacher-Trainer in Thailand, a Beverage Manager in the UK, an Information Officer for the United Nations and a Wine Columnist for CBC radio in Canada. Troy has won many awards for his writing including a prestigious 'Travel Writer of the Year' award with TNT Magazine UK and a "Gourmand World Cookbook Award".

Troy fell in love with a Canadian girl, married her and then fell in love with Canada, his new home.

ABOUT THE ILLUSTRATOR

Jennifer Sara Harrington is a graphic designer and illustrator with eight years of experience working in the publishing industry. Born in Vancouver, she completed an Anthropology degree before pursuing a career in graphic design. She has worked on numerous Canadian publications including Wedding Bells, Vancouver Lifestyles Magazine, Canadian Traveller, Travel & More and Tribute Magazine.

She spent two years working in London, England as a Magazine Designer and Art Director for several top contract publishing companies in the city. A self-trained artist, she has created murals, portraits, book covers and children's book illustrations for a broad range of clientele.

She currently works as a designer at a clothing and accessories company in Toronto, Ontario. This is her first fully illustrated children's book.

www.amooseinamapletree.com